My "k" Sound Box®

Library of Congress Cataloging-in-Publication Data
Moncure, Jane Belk.
My "k" sound box / by Jane Belk Moncure; illustrated by Colin King.
p. cm.
Summary: A little boy fills his sound box with many words beginning with the letter "k."
ISBN 1-56766-777-5 (lib. bdg. : alk. paper)
[1. Alphabet.] I. King, Colin, ill. II. Title.
PZ7.M739 Myk   2000
[E]—dc21   99-055423

My "k" Sound Box

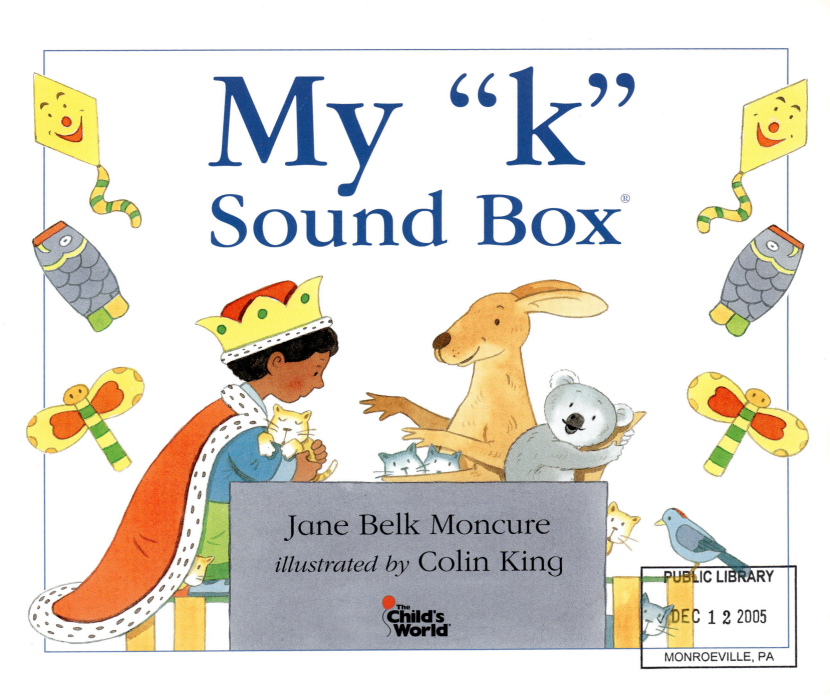

Jane Belk Moncure

illustrated by Colin King

The Child's World®

Little  had a box.

"I will find things that begin with my 'k' sound," he said.

"I will put them into my sound box."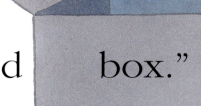

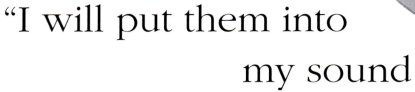

"But first, I will be a king."

So he dressed up as a king.

Then Little  went for a walk.

He found a koala.

Did he put the koala into his box?
He did.

Next, Little  found

kingbirds.

Did he put the kingbirds
into his box? He did.

Then Little  found a kitty.

"Kitty, kitty," he called.

Lots and lots of kittens came . . .

from everywhere!

Little  tried to put the kittens into the box. But the kingbirds did not like it!

Do you know why?

What could Little  do?

He found a . . .

kangaroo.

The kangaroo had a big pocket.

Little  put all the kittens
into the pocket.

"A king can do anything!"
said Little

So he played the kettledrum.
Then he put it into the box.

Next, he looked through a kaleidoscope.

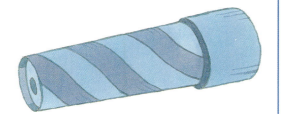

Here is what he saw.

He put the kaleidoscope into the box, too.

Then Little  found kites,

lots and lots of kites.

"I will fly a kite," he said.

But the wind blew the kite away.
The kingbirds flew after the kite.

The kittens kicked the kangaroo.

The kangaroo sneezed, "Kerchoo!"
and blew . . .

everything into a . . .

kindergarten.

My, what fun the children had!

kites

kingbirds

kitten

kettledrum

kingbird

kitten

kangaroo

koala

kittens

kaleidoscope

kitten

Can you read these words
with Little  ?

kiss

keg

katydid

ketchup

kettle

key

kitchen

kid

kid

kimono

kayak

29

ABOUT THE AUTHOR AND ILLUSTRATOR

Jane Belk Moncure began her writing career when she was in kindergarten. She has never stopped writing. Many of her children's stories and poems have been published, to the delight of young readers, including her son Jim, whose childhood experiences found their way into many of her books.

Mrs. Moncure's writing is based upon an active career in early childhood education. A recipient of an M.A. degree from Columbia University, Mrs. Moncure has taught and directed nursery, kindergarten, and primary grade programs in California, New York, Virginia, and North Carolina. As a former member of the faculties of Virginia Commonwealth University and the University of Richmond, she taught prospective teachers in early childhood education.

Mrs. Moncure has travelled extensively abroad, studying early childhood programs in the United Kingdom, The Netherlands, and Switzerland. She was the first president of the Virginia Association for Early Childhood Education and received its award for outstanding service to young children.

A resident of North Carolina, Mrs. Moncure is currently a full-time writer and educational consultant. She is married to Dr. James A. Moncure, former vice president of Elon College.

Colin King studied at the Royal College of Art, London. He started his freelance career as an illustrator, working for magazines and advertising agencies.

He began drawing pictures for children's books in 1976 and has illustrated over sixty titles to date.

Included in a wide variety of subjects are a best-selling children's encyclopedia and books about spies and detectives.

His books have been translated into several languages, including Japanese and Hebrew. He has four grown-up children and lives in Suffolk, England, with his wife, three dogs, and a cat.